Catherine Patricia Cox

"COME NOW, TELL ME ALL ABOUT IT AND HOW IT HAPPENED."

MONI
THE GOAT BOY

By
JOHANNA SPYRI
The Author of "Heidi"

Translated By
CLEMENT W. COUMBE

Illustrated By
FRANCES BRUNDAGE

THE
SAALFIELD PUBLISHING COMPANY
AKRON, OHIO NEW YORK

Made in U. S. A.

PREFACE

The first few pages of any one of the children's stories written by Johanna Spyri are sufficient to draw one into the circle of her admirers.

Born in the quaint little town of Hirzel in the heights of the Swiss Alps, Madam Spyri lived the life about which she has written so interestingly. She loved her Switzerland; she loved and understood children. Her stories about both are unexcelled in literature.

This charming story of the simple-hearted peasant lad who lived true to his ideals is as delightful as the longer story of "Heidi" which has captivated so many thousands of children.

FULL-PAGE ILLUSTRATIONS

MONI
THE GOAT BOY

CHAPTER I

ALL IS WELL WITH MONI

To reach the Inn at Fideris Springs one must follow a long steep road which leads out of the beautiful valley of Prättigau. The fact is, the horses pant so in their toil up the mountain grade that many travelers prefer getting out of the coach and climbing to the green heights on foot.

After a long ascent the village of Fideris is

reached on its friendly green knoll, and from there you press on into the very heart of the mountains until the lonesome Inn of the bathing resort comes into sight, all surrounded by rocky heights. Here and there grow the fir trees which clothe the summit rocks, and it would be a gloomy spot indeed did not the mountain flowers peep through the pasture grass and show their brilliant colors.

One clear summer evening two ladies stepped out of the Inn and followed the narrow pathway which soon commences to rise and quickly climbs steeply up to the towering cliffs. At the **first** projecting ledge they paused to gaze at the view, for they had only just arrived at the Baths.

"It's not very gay up here, Auntie," remarked the younger, as she let her eyes range around. "Nothing but rocks and fir forests, then a mountain and more firs on it. If we have to remain here for six weeks, I do wish there was something more amusing to look at."

"It won't make for amusement, Paula, if you lose your diamond cross here," replied the aunt as she fastened the red satin ribbon on which the girl wore a sparkling cross. "This is the third

time I have tied your ribbon since we arrived. I do not know if the fault lies with you or the ribbon, but I do know that you will make a great to-do if the cross is lost."

"No, no!" was the quick exclamation of Paula. "The cross must not be lost on any account! It was my grandmother's and is my dearest treasure." Paula now seized the ribbon and tied two, three knots, one after the other, so as to make it secure. Suddenly she pricked up her ears and said eagerly, "Listen, listen, Auntie! Now actually comes something amusing!"

From high above them resounded a joyous song. Then came a long ringing yodel*, followed by the song again. The ladies looked up but could discover no living being. The foot-path ran in long curves, often between high bushes and again between projecting mountain slopes, so that, looking upward, there were only broken glimpses of the path. But suddenly all

---

*The yodel is a kind of thrilling refrain used by the Swiss herdsmen with their songs.

was alive on the trail; above and below, in every place where the narrow path was visible, while ever louder and nearer rang the song.

"Look, look, Auntie! There, there! Look there, just look!" cried Paula in amusement; and to the intense delight of both ladies, there came hither three, then four goats springing down the path, then more, ever more. And each goat had a tiny bell around its neck, which tinkled at every movement. In the midst of the flock was the goat boy leaping along and singing the last verse of his song:

> "I'm never sad in winter,
> But always glad and gay,
> For the bright and merry springtime
> Will soon be on its way."

Then he let out a powerful yodel, and stood with his flock close to the ladies, for with his bare feet he sprang as nimbly and softly as the mountain goats.

"I wish you good evening!" said he, giving the couple a gay glance and he would have proceeded

2

on his way, but the goat boy with happy eyes pleased the ladies and Paula said, "Wait a bit! Are you the goat boy from Fideris? Have you the goats from the village below?"

"Yes, surely!" was the answer.

"And do you go up the mountain with them every day?" she continued.

"Yes, certainly."

"And what is your name?"

"I am called Moni."

"Will you sing again the song that you have just sung? We heard only one stanza."

"It is too long," declared Moni, "the goats must be home before it is too late," and he straightened his weather-worn cap, swung his rod in the air and called the goats together with, "Home! home!" for they had started to nibble everywhere.

"But you will sing it to me some other time, Moni, won't you?" called Paula after him.

"Why, yes, that I will, and good-night!" the goat boy called back as he started on a trot with

MONI, THE GOAT BOY

THERE CAME HITHER THREE, THEN FOUR GOATS SPRINGING DOWN THE PATH. IN THE MIDST WAS THE GOAT BOY.

his goats, and in a little while the entire flock
paused by the out-building which stood a few
feet behind the Inn at the Springs, for it was
here that Moni daily left the pretty white goat
and the black one with the delicate little kid, for
those three belonged to the Inn. The dainty kid
Moni handled with greatest care, for it was a
weak creature and he loved it above all the
others. It was so dependent upon him and followed him about all day long. Now he led it
gently to the shed and placed it in its stall, saying, "Now, Mäggerli, sleep well; you must be
tired. It is a long way up the mountain, and you
so small. Lie right down, see, so—right in the
nice straw!"

After having bedded Mäggerli, Moni hurried
along with his flock, first to the hill in front of
the Inn, and then down the steep road to the
village. Approaching the little town, he took
out his Alpine horn and blew a powerful blast
upon it, until it resounded far into the valley
beneath. At this signal from the scattered

dwellings came children on the run, each seizing his own goat which he knew from a great distance. From some of the nearby houses came a woman here, and another there, taking her little goat by the string or by the horns, and in a short time the entire flock was separated, each goat going to its owner. Last of all, Moni stood alone

with Brownie, his own, and with her went to the
cottage on the mountain slope where his grandmother stood in the doorway awaiting him.

"Has everything gone well, Moni?" she asked

kindly and then without waiting for his answer
she led Brownie to her shed and at once began to
milk her.

The grandmother was still a robust woman
and took care of everything herself, both in the
house and in the shed, and all was in good order.
Moni stood at the shed door and watched as she

milked. When the task was finished, she stepped into the cottage and said, "Come, Moni; you must be hungry."

The evening meal was prepared, and Moni had nothing to do but sit down at the table, his grandmother alongside of him. The fare was frugal—nothing but a bowl of cornmeal mush cooked in Brownie's milk, but to Moni it was delicious. While they ate, Moni related to the grandmother all his experiences of the day and as soon as the meal was over he went to his bed, for he had to be out again at dawn with his flock.

Two summers had already passed Moni after

this manner, and he had become so accustomed to his life as goat boy and had grown so attached to the goats that he could not think of life being otherwise. Moni had lived with his grandmother as long as he could remember. His mother had died when he was just a little lad, and soon afterwards his father went away with others to Naples to serve in the army, so as to be earning something, he said, for he thought things would go better there. His wife's mother was also poor, but she took her daughter's forsaken little child, the young Solomon, or Moni, as he was called, into her care and shared with him what she had. Her unselfishness brought a blessing on her cottage and she had never known what it was to suffer want.

The brave old Grandmother Elsbeth was well liked by everybody in the village, and two years before when a new goat boy was to be named for the hamlet, all voices were raised in favor of Moni, for no one begrudged the hard-working Elsbeth the pennies Moni would earn.

The pious grandmother never permitted Moni to go out to work a single morning without reminding him: "Moni, don't forget when you are up there how near you are to the beloved God, and that He sees and hears everything. You can hide nothing from His eyes. Also forget not that He is near to help you; you need

never be afraid. If no man is within call, just ask the dear God when in need and He will hear you at once and will come to your aid."

And thus from the very first Moni went forth in full reliance and never had the slightest fear or dread up on the lonesome peaks and the highest rocks, for he always thought: "The higher up I go, the nearer I am to God, and I am that much safer whatsoever happens to me."

So Moni had neither care nor worry and rejoiced in everything he did from morn till eve, and it was no wonder he was constantly whistling, singing and yodeling, for he had to give vent to his great happiness.

CHAPTER II

THE following morning Paula awoke earlier than ever before, for a lusty song roused her out of her sleep.

"There's the goat boy for sure!" she exclaimed as she sprang out of bed and went to her window.

And, sure enough, Moni stood below, his cheeks all rosy with the climb, and beside him

was the old goat and the kid he had just led out
of the Inn shed. Now, as he swung his rod in
the air, the goats danced and leaped around him

in impatience to be off. Suddenly Moni raised
his voice in song and as they started for the
pastures, the mountains flung back the echo:

"High on the tops of the fir-trees
  The birds so merrily sing;
For after the rain the sun will shine
  Like a great majestic king."

"Today he must sing the entire song for me,"
said Paula, for now Moni had disappeared and

she could not understand the rest of the words.

The rosy clouds of morning flushed the heavens and a fresh mountain breeze rustled around Moni's head as he climbed upward. The new day just suited him, and in his keen enjoyment of it when he reached the first ledge of rock, he yodelled so loudly that far down at the Inn many a sleeping guest opened his eyes in astonishment, then quickly closed them again as he recognized the sound and knew he could claim another hour of slumber. Everyone who stayed at the Inn for any time at all grew familiar with the voice of the goat boy, who always came by so early.

Meanwhile Moni and his goats climbed up and up for another hour, and with every step the view spread wider before them and grew in beauty. From time to time Moni gazed into the clear sky above which became bluer and bluer; next, full-throated, he commenced to sing, ever louder and more joyfully the higher he climbed:

"High on the tops of the fir-trees
　　The birds so merrily sing;
For after the rain the sun will shine
　　Like a great majestic king.

The sun shines brightly through the day,
　　The moon and stars at night—
Our dear Lord made them all for us
　　To give us great delight.

The flowers all come in the springtime,
　　The violet, rose and bluebell,
And the sky is so bright and blue then
　　My gladness I scarcely can tell.

And when berries come in summer
　　I pick them all with glee,
The juicy red and black ones
　　Make a splendid feast for me.

In fall the nuts I gather
　　Which I know where to find,
And there I take my goats to eat
　　Good herbs of every kind.

And I'm never sad in winter
　　But always glad and gay
For the bright and merry springtime
　　Will soon be on its way."

Now the height was reached where Moni usually tarried for the day, and where he planned to spend this one. It was a small green tableland and there was a wide projecting rock where one could, from this free point, see all around and likewise deep down into the valley. This projection was known as the Pulpit Rock, and here Moni would stay for hours at a time, gazing about and whistling away while his goats contentedly hunted for herbage round about.

As soon as Moni arrived, he took his haversack off his back and put it in a little hollow in the ground which he had dug for this particular purpose. Then he stepped out on the Pulpit Rock and threw himself down on the earth intending to enjoy life to the utmost.

The sky had deepened into a most wonderfully dark blue. Opposite where Moni lay, the high mountains stretched up their jagged peaks to pierce the sky, and their great fields of ice dazzled the eye, while below, far as one could

see, the green valley was touched by the morning glow.

Moni lay gazing on all this grandeur and sang and whistled in deep contentment. The mountain breeze cooled his heated brow and when he stopped whistling the birds above him sang more merrily than he, as they soared into the blue. The goat boy was unspeakably happy.

From time to time Mäggerli came alongside him and rubbed her head on his shoulder for sheer tenderness, then bleated affectionately and walked around him to repeat the muzzling on his other shoulder. Of the others, first one, then another came to look at their herder and each had its own way of paying its visit.

Brownie, Moni's own goat, came with evident anxiety and looked around to see if all was well with him. She stood close by and gazed at him until he said, "Yes, yes, Brownie, everything's all right! Go back to your forage."

A young white goat and one named Swallow, because she was so slender and agile and darted so swiftly here, there and everywhere like the swallows flying into their holes, always made their visit together. They rushed up against Moni with such force that they would have knocked him over had he not already been stretched full length on the ground, and shot away as swiftly as they came.

The shiny Blackie, Mäggerli's mother, who

3

belonged to the landlord of the Fideris Inn,
was rather proud. She came no nearer than a
few feet, looked at Moni with uplifted head as
though she did not wish to appear too intimate,
then leisurely went her way again. But the
great Sultan, the ram, did not approach more
than once a day, and then shoved away any goat
he found near Moni with an air of great im-
portance and gave forth several bleats as though
imparting information about the condition of
the flock, whose leader he felt himself to be.

Little Mäggerli alone never allowed Big Sultan
to crowd her away from her protector. If the
big billy-goat came while she was with the goat
boy she crept under his arm, so that it was quite

impossible for Big Sultan to reach her. Under Moni's protection the little kid was not one whit afraid of him, though if he had come near her when alone she would have trembled with fright.

Thus the sunny morning waned. Moni had eaten his midday repast and now stood leaning thoughtfully on his staff, which he often needed up here for it made his climbing up and down very easy. He was trying to decide whether or not he would climb up a new side of the rock, for he wished to go higher this afternoon with the goats. The only question was which side. He decided in favor of the left, for there around the three Dragon Stones grew such tender bushes as

would offer a true banquet for the goats.

The way was steep and above there were dangerous places on the bluff rock wall. But Moni knew the path and the goats had too much sense to go astray. So he started clambering and all his goats climbed eagerly, some before, some after him. But the little Mäggerli kept close at his side. When they came to the steepest places he took hold of her and often pulled her along to safety.

All went well and now they were at the summit. With great leaps the goats ran at once to the green bushes, for they well knew the excellent herbage they had frequently nibbled up here.

"Tame yourselves! Tame yourselves!" warned Moni. "Don't butt yourselves over the cliffs! In a single moment one of you could easily tumble over and break your bones. Swallow! Swallow! What has entered your brain?" he cried in excitement and fear, for the agile goat had climbed over the high Dragon Stones and now stood on the outer ledge, peeping pertly down on him. He climbed up with all the swiftness he could summon, for he knew it needed just one false step for Swallow to lie in the abyss

below. Moni was very nimble and in a few minutes had climbed the stone and seizing Swallow's leg had dragged her back to safety. "Now come with me, you senseless creature!" scolded Moni, leading her down to the other goats and being careful to hold her for awhile until she had nibbled at the bushes and he was convinced she had no more thought of running away.

"Where is Mäggerli?" Moni suddenly cried

out when he noticed Blackie as she stood alone on a steep place eating nothing but looking all round. The young kid was always either alongside Moni or running after Blackie, its mother.

"Where is your little kid, Blackie?" Moni asked in alarm and sprang towards the goat. She acted quite strangely. She ate nothing and stayed always on the same spot and pricked up her ears suspiciously. Moni came close to her and looked above and below. Now he heard a gentle, plaintive bleating. That was Mäggerli's voice! It came from below, so pitiful and pleading for help. Moni threw himself on the ground and peered over. There was a movement; now he saw it plainly. Far below Mäggerli hung from the branch of a tree that grew out of the rocks and her crying went straight to Moni's heart. She must have fallen over the edge and fortunately the branch had caught her. Otherwise she would have plunged into the abyss and met a pitiful death. But even now if she lost her hold, she would crash down into the depths and be dashed to pieces.

In greatest anguish Moni called down: "Hold firm, Mäggerli! Hold tight to the branch! See, I am coming and will fetch you!"

But how should he reach her? The wall of rock was so perpendicular, it was quite clear to

Moni that to clamber down was an impossibility. Then he remembered the Rain Rock, that projecting ledge under which he so safely sought refuge from the storms; it was here goat boys for years and years had spent their time in bad weather. In fact, it had received its name of Rain Rock ever so long ago because of this. Little Mäggerli must be down near the level of the Rain Rock, thought Moni, and he believed he could climb straight across the ledge and thus rescue the little kid.

Quickly he whistled his flock together and descended with his goats to the entrance of the Rain Rock. Here he left them to graze while he began his perilous task of rescue. He could see little Mäggerli, not so very far away from him now but in a perilous position hanging to the branch of the tree. He saw too that it would not be easy to climb up there and then return with Mäggerli on his back. But there was no other way of saving the little creature.

Now he recalled the daily words of his grandmother: that the good Lord was always with him so that he could not fail in any task. He folded his hands, gazed up to heaven and prayed:

"O dear God, do help me so I can rescue Mäggerli!"

The prayer filled him with confidence that all would go well, and sturdily he clambered up the cliff until he reached the tree. Gripping firmly with both feet, he lifted the trembling, whimpering little creature to his shoulders and began the descent with the greatest caution. When he again found himself on the firm grassy soil and

saw the little goat safe, he was so happy he had to utter aloud his thanks and cry out to heaven: "O dear God, I thank Thee a thousand times for helping us so well! Oh, how grateful both of us are!" Then he sat down on the ground, drew the little kid to him and gently stroked its trembling limbs and consoled it for the terror it had endured.

Very soon it was time to depart, and Moni put the little kid over his shoulders again and said

As Paula listened to the story, she stroked the little animal that now lay restfully across Moni's knee.

tenderly: "Come, you poor little Mäggerli, you are still trembling; you cannot walk home. I must carry you," and with the little creature clinging close to him, he took his downward way.

Paula and her aunt were awaiting the goat boy on the first rise above the Fideris Inn, and when Moni appeared with the burden on his back, Paula wanted to know whether or not the little kid was sick, and showed great sympathy. When Moni saw her interest, he seated himself on the ground in front of her and related his day's experience with Mäggerli. As Paula listened intently to the story, she stroked the little animal that now lay restfully across Moni's knees, looking very pretty with its white feet and shining black back. It seemed quite pleased to receive her gentle petting.

"Now then, you will please sing your song for me while you are sitting here so comfortably," said Paula.

Moni was in such a happy humor that he struck up full chested and sang the song from beginning to end. Paula was delighted and declared he must sing it to her often, and then the entire party walked down to the Inn together. Here little Mäggerli was placed on her straw bed, Moni bade her good-night and then hurried on to the village, while Paula returned to her room with her aunt, where she talked a long time about the goat boy and his song that she had so enjoyed.

CHAPTER III
A VISIT

SEVERAL days passed, one as bright and sunny as the other for this was a specially beautiful summer and not a cloud flecked the blue of the sky from morn to eve.

Starting out very early each morning, the goat boy passed the Inn singing his ringing song. Every evening in full song he returned, and all the guests at the Inn grew so accustomed to the merry music that none would have cared to miss it. But Paula more than all the others delighted in Moni's happiness, and went out to meet him almost every evening in order to have a little chat with him.

One sunshiny morning Moni had gone up to the Pulpit Rock and was just ready to throw himself down on the ground as usual when he suddenly changed his mind.

"No, forward!" he called to his goats. "The last time you were high up, you had to leave the tender young leaves because we had to rescue Mäggerli. Now we will go up again and you can finish nibbling them."

Joyfully the goats all sprang after him, for

they noticed they were going in the direction of the Dragon Stones and the fine bushes that grew around them. But this time Moni held his little Mäggerli in his arms all the time, feeding her out of his hand with the leaves he plucked from the bushes that grew on the rocks. This seemed to the little goat the very best thing that could happen, and to show her contentment she rubbed her little head on Moni's shoulder and bleated happily.

Thus the whole morning passed before Moni noticed how hungry he had grown and so knew it must be late. But he had left his dinner bag down below in the little hollow at the Pulpit Rock for he had expected to return there at midday.

"Come now, all of you have had a good time feeding and I have had nothing," said he to his goats. "I too must have something to eat and you will find more for yourselves down below. Come!" Therewith he gave a loud whistle and at the signal the whole flock was up and away,

the liveliest always in front.   The nimble-footed
Swallow led the way, and was to meet an unex-
pected adventure this day.   She sprang down
from stone to stone and over many a crevice, but
suddenly she paused—she could go no farther,

for a chamois stood directly in front of her and
gazed into her face in surprised curiosity.   Such
a thing had never happened to Swallow before!
She stood stock still, looked doubtfully at the
stranger and waited for him to get out of her
path so she could leap to the next crag as she

4

had intended. To her amazement he did not waver, but stared impudently at her. Thus they faced one another, both obstinate, and might have stood there to this very day had not the Big Sultan come along. Directly he saw the state of affairs, he stepped past Swallow and gave the chamois such a powerful push to one side that it had to make a daring leap to save itself from a disastrous fall down over the rocks. Swallow now triumphantly wended her way downward, while Sultan stepped along proudly behind her, with a self-satisfied air, for he felt he was the true protector of the goats of his flock.

As Moni and his goats were descending, another goat boy was climbing up, and when they met both lads showed astonishment at the encounter, but as they knew one another well they exchanged friendly greetings. The climber was Jörgli of Küblis. He had been searching vainly for Moni half the day, and now found him in the heights where he had little expected he would be.

"I thought you never went so high up with the goats," said Jörgli.

"Sometimes I do, but not often," replied Moni. "Generally I am near the Pulpit Rock, or a little above it. Why did you come up here?"

"I wanted to pay you a visit," was the reply. "I have all sorts of things to tell you. Besides, I have two goats here which I am taking to the landlord at the Inn. He wishes to buy one and so I thought I would come up to see you."

"Are they your goats?" asked Moni.

"Of course they are ours. I don't have to tend strange ones; I am no longer a goat boy."

This news set Moni wondering, for Jörgli had been made goat boy for Küblis at the same time Moni had been chosen goat boy for Fideris, and he could not understand how Jörgli could give up his work without even a murmur.

In the meantime both goat boys and their flocks had reached the Pulpit Rock. Moni brought out his bread and dried meat and invited Jörgli to share his dinner. Seating themselves out on the Pulpit Rock, they did full justice to the occasion, for it was getting late and both had ravenous appetites. When all was eaten and then a little goat's milk drunk, Jörgli stretched himself comfortably at full length on the ground and rested his head on both arms; but Moni remained sitting on the Rock, for he loved to gaze into the valley deep below.

"What are you doing then, Jörgli, if you are no longer goat boy?" began Moni. "You must be doing something."

"Certainly I am doing something, and some-

thing fine," replied Jörgli. "I am egg boy. Every day I carry eggs to all the hotels round about, going just as far as I can; I come up to the Fideris Springs Inn—I was there yesterday."

Moni shook his head. "That's nothing. I wouldn't care to be an egg boy. I would a thousand times sooner be a goat boy. That is ever so much nicer!"

"Yes? Why do you think so?"

"Eggs are not alive, you can't talk to them, and they can't run after you the way the goats do, and they cannot be happy when you come, and grow fond of you and understand every word you say to them. You can't have any joy over your eggs like you can with the goats," explained Moni.

"And what about yourself?" interrupted Jörgli. "What great fun do you have up here? Just now you have had to jump up six times while we were eating to go after a stupid little goat to keep it from falling below. Do you call that fun?"

"Yes, I am glad to do that!" Then, "What's the matter, Mäggerli? Come, come!" he exclaimed, and for the seventh time Moni jumped up and ran after the little goat, for its frantic leaps of joy might lead it into danger. When he sat down again, Jörgli said:

"There is a way for holding young goats so they don't tumble off the cliffs and one does not have to keep eternally jumping after them like you do."

"What way?" asked Moni.

"You drive a stick fast in the ground and tie the goat to it by one leg. Of course it struggles fearfully, but it can't get away."

"You have no idea I would do anything like that with my little kid, have you?" said Moni quite angrily as he drew Mäggerli to him and held the little goat close as though protecting it from any such treatment.

"Well, you certainly won't have to worry much longer about that one," Jörgli began again. "It won't come up here many more times."

"What's that you say? What? Jörgli, what are you saying?" said Moni excitedly.

"Pshaw! Don't you know? The innkeeper at the Baths doesn't want to rear it because it is too sickly and will never grow to be a strong goat. He wanted to sell it to my father, but he didn't want it either. Now the landlord is going to slaughter it next week, and then he will buy our piebald goat there."

Moni's face turned white with dismay. At first he could not utter one word, but suddenly he broke out into loud sobs over his little kid.

"No, no! They mustn't do that! Mäggerli, they must not do it! They must not kill you! I could not stand it! Oh, I would rather die with you! No, that cannot be!"

"Don't carry on so," said Jörgli angrily, pulling Moni up, for in his grief the goat boy had thrown himself face downward on the ground. "Stand up! You know well enough that the little goat belongs to the landlord and he can do just what he pleases with it. Think no more about it! Come, I know something else. Just look at this!" And with these words Jörgli held out one hand to Moni though he nearly covered with his other hand the object Moni was to admire. In spite of his care something sparkled wonderfully as the sun's rays shone upon it.

"What is it?" asked Moni, as it blazed again when lit up by the rays of the sun.

"Guess!"

"A ring?"

"No, but something of that sort."

"Who gave it to you?"

"Gave it to me? No one did—I found it myself."

"But then it does not belong to you, Jörgli."

"Why not? I did not take it from anybody. Instead, I almost trod on it. Then it would have been broken; I can just as well keep it."

"Where did you find it?"

"Down below near the Inn, last evening."

"Then someone at the Inn must have lost it.

You must tell the landlord. If you don't, I'll have to do so this evening."

"No, no, Moni, don't do that!" pleaded Jörgli. "See, I will show you what it is. I am going to sell it to some chambermaid at one of the hotels. I'll certainly get four francs for it. Then I'll give you one or two. No one will know anything about it."

"I don't want any money! I won't take it!" interrupted Moni. "And the dear God has heard every word you have said."

Jörgli looked up at the sky. "Yes? So far away?" he said doubtfully; but at once he lowered his voice in talking.

"He hears you just the same," declared Moni, with assurance.

Jörgli was growing very uncomfortable. If he could only bring Moni over to his side! If not, everything was lost. He thought and thought. "Moni," he proposed suddenly, "if you will tell no one about what I have found, I will promise you something that will please you.

You need not take any money, so you will have nothing to do with it. If you will promise to do as I wish, I will arrange it so that my father buys Mäggerli, and the little kid will not be slaughtered after all. Will you do it?"

A hard struggle went on in Moni. He knew it was wrong to help to keep secret the finding of the precious object. Jörgli had opened his hand, and in it lay a cross set with many stones which reflected beautiful colors. Moni realized this was no worthless thing; he felt sure someone would seek for it. If he remained silent, it was as though he himself held what did not belong to him. On the other hand, there was the little loving Mäggerli who would be killed by a frightful knife. He could save her if he would keep silent. Even then the little goat lay alongside him as though she knew he would always help her. No, he could not let it happen—he must help to save her!

"I'll do it, Jörgli," he said, but without any pleasure.

"Give me your hand on it!" and Jörgli grasped it, that Moni should promise on it for only thus was a promise unbreakable.

Jörgli was very happy now that he felt the matter was settled as he wished, but as Moni had grown so quiet he thought he had a good excuse to get away because his home was much farther off than Moni's. Saying good-bye to Moni, he whistled his two fellow-travelers to his side, for meanwhile they had made companions of Moni's browsing goats, though not without several attacks taking place between the two parties.

The Fideris goats had not yet learned that during a visit they should behave in a mannerly way, and the Küblis goats did not know that when they were visitors they should not hunt the best herbage and push others away.

When Jörgli had gone a short distance below, Moni began his departure with his flock, but he kept quite silent, singing not a note and letting out not a single little whistle all the way home.

CHAPTER IV

NO LONGER CAN MONI SING

THE morning following Jörgli's visit Moni went up the path to the Baths as silently and dejectedly as he had descended the evening before. Quietly he fetched out the landlord's goats and climbed farther up the heights. He did not sing a note, did not yodel up into the air, but walked with hanging head and forlorn face as though he feared something. Now and then he looked around shyly as if half expecting to find someone following who wished to question him.

Moni had lost his merry heart, he did not know exactly why. He wanted to feel pleased that he had saved little Mäggerli but when he tried to sing, the words would not come forth. The sky was hidden by clouds and Moni thought if the sun would come out he would feel differently and be merry enough.

As he gained the heights above it began to

rain very hard and he sought shelter under the Rain Rock, for it had become a downpour. The goats followed and took refuge with him under the Rock. Indeed, the genteel Blackie crept under the Rock even before Moni to protect her beautiful shiny coat, and now she sat down behind him and looked out contentedly from her comfortable corner, watching the pouring rain. Little Mäggerli stood in front of her protector under the projecting rock and gently rubbed her little head against his knees. When this affectionate act brought no friendly word from Moni, Mäggerli looked up at him in surprise, for she was not accustomed to such silence. Deep in thought, Moni sat there leaning on the staff which he always carried in such rainy weather

to prevent him from slipping on the dangerously steep places, for on such days he wore shoes. There he sat under the Rain Rock, hour after hour in deep reflection.

Moni pondered over his promise to Jörgli. It

seemed to him as though Jörgli had taken something and he was as guilty as Jörgli because he
had been given something as a reward for keep-
ing silent. Certainly he had done wrong and he
felt in his heart the good Lord was displeased
with him. He felt it was right that the day was
dark and rainy and that he should hide under the
rock for he would not have dared to look up into
the clear blue sky; he was afraid of the good Lord.

But there were still other things Moni had to
think about that day: if Mäggerli were to fall
down over the steep cliff now, and he wished to
rescue her and the good Lord would not protect
him, and he dared no longer pray to Him, and so
was not safe; and if he slipped and fell with
Mäggerli down over the jagged rocks and lay
shattered in the abyss—Oh no! he said in
anguish of heart, it must not come to this! He
must make matters so he could pray again and
go to the good Lord with everything that lay
next to his heart. Only then could he be happy.

He wanted to throw off this load that pressed him down. He would go and tell the landlord everything—but what would happen then? Jörgli would not persuade his father and the landlord would slaughter little Mäggerli. "Oh, no! Oh no!" he exclaimed in desperation. He could not bear that. "I won't do it; I'll say nothing!" But this decision brought him no relief; the weight on his heart grew heavier and heavier. And thus Moni passed the day. He returned home songless, as he had come in the morning. And when Paula waited for him at the Inn and came hurriedly to him to the goat shed and asked tenderly, "Moni, what ails you? Why don't you sing any more?" he turned shyly away and said, "I can't," and made off with his goats as quickly as possible.

"If only I knew what is the matter with the goat boy!" said Paula to her aunt. "Such a change has come over him, one would hardly know him. If only he would sing again!"

"It is the dismal rain that has put him out of

sorts," was the opinion of the older woman.

"Everything comes upon us at once! Let us go home, Auntie!" Paula begged. "The fun is over here. First I lose my lovely cross and it can not be found. Then comes this endless rain and now one cannot even hear the merry goat boy. Do let us get away!"

"The course at the Baths must be carried out. Nothing must interfere with that," declared the aunt.

The next morning dawned dark and gray and the rain streamed down unceasingly. Moni passed the hours under the Rain Rock, exactly as he had the day before. There he sat disconsolately. His thoughts roamed restlessly in circles, for when he once made up his mind, "Now I'll go and confess the wrong, so I may look up to the dear Lord again," then he saw before him the little Mäggerli under the cruel knife, and the debate would begin all over again. Thus with thinking and brooding over the troubles he carried, he was over-weary by evening and crept home in the streaming rain as though he did not even notice it.

The landlord was standing in the rear doorway at the Inn as Moni came by and called roughly to him, "Get along with you, the goats are surely wet enough! Why do you crawl down the mountain like a snail? I am beginning to wonder what's the matter with you."

The landlord had never been so gruff with Moni before. Quite the contrary, he had always greeted the happy goat boy with a kindly word. But Moni's changed manner did not please him

at all. Besides, he was in a bad humor because Miss Paula had complained to him of her loss and declared firmly that the expensive cross could only have been lost in the hotel or directly in front of the inn door, for on the day it had disappeared she had not stepped outside except to listen for the song of the goat boy as he came home. That anyone could say a valuable could be lost in his hotel without it being found made him very savage. Only the day before he had summoned all his servants, had examined and cross-examined them, threatened and at last offered a reward to the finder of the cross. The whole Inn was in an uproar over the lost jewel.

As Moni passed in front of the Inn with his goats, Paula was standing there as usual. She had been waiting for him, wondering if he would be silent and gloomy, or able to sing as in the old days. As he would have crept by without a word, she called out: "Moni! Moni! Are you really the same goat boy who used to sing from morning till evening:

'The flowers all come in the springtime,
The violet, rose and bluebell,
And the sky is so bright and blue then
My gladness I scarcely can tell.'"

Moni heard her words, and though he gave no answer, they made a deep impression on him. Oh, how different it was when he could sing the livelong day and feel exactly as he sang! Oh, if only that time would come again!

The next day Moni mounted the heights, silent,

cheerless and without song. The rain was over
at last, but the mists hung in gloom on the mountains and the heavens were still dark with gray
clouds. Sitting under the Rain Rock, Moni
struggled with his thoughts. Towards midday

the clouds began to lift and the sky grew brighter and brighter. Moni came forward out of the cave and looked around. The goats leaped joyfully here and there; even the little kid was quite saucy with happiness over the returning sun and frolicked about.

Moni stood outside on the Pulpit Rock and watched the day brighten on the mountains beyond and saw the valley below grow beautiful. The clouds parted and the blue sky peeped down so friendly and full of charm that Moni felt as if God looked down on him right out of the blue. Suddenly it came to him quite clearly what he must do. He could not carry the weight of that wrong around with him a day longer; he must throw it off. Quickly Moni seized the little goat that was frolicking around him, took it up into his arms and said tenderly:

"Oh, Mäggerli, you poor Mäggerli! I have certainly done all I could, but I cannot do wrong. Oh, if you only did not have to die! I cannot stand it!" And now Moni began to cry so that he could not speak any more and the little kid bleated mournfully and crept under his arm as if it sought safety and protection there. "Come, Mäggerli, I'll carry you home once more today; I'll not be able to carry you many more times."

When the flock came to the Inn, Paula was standing there on watch. Moni placed the young Mäggerli with Blackie in the stall and then instead of going on down to the village, Moni turned toward Paula and was going past her to the Inn but she detained him with: "Still songless, Moni? Where are you going with your sorrowful face?"

"I have to report something to the landlord,"

answered Moni without lifting his eyes.

"Report something! What is it? May I not know?"

"I must go to the landlord. Something has been found."

"Found? What is it? I have lost something —a beautiful cross."

"Yes, that's just what it is."

"What do you tell me?" cried Paula in the greatest surprise. "Is it a cross with sparkling stones?"

"Yes, just so."

"What have you done with it, then, Moni? Give it to me! Did you find it?"

"No; Jörgli of Küblis did."

Then Paula wanted to know who Jörgli was and where he lived, and she planned to send someone down at Küblis at once to fetch the cross.

"I'll hurry down there and if he still has it, I'll bring it back," said Moni.

"If he still has it?" cried Paula. "Why

shouldn't he have it ? And how do you come to know all about it? When did he find it and how did you learn of it?"

Moni stared at the ground. He did not dare tell how everything had happened and how he had helped to keep the discovery a secret until he could bear it no longer. But Paula must have understood and she drew him to her side and they seated themselves on the trunk of a tree as she said to him in the most friendly manner: "Come now, tell me all about it and how it happened, Moni. I would be so glad to know everything from you."

Paula's sympathy gave Moni confidence and he told the whole story, relating his struggle on account of Mäggerli and how all his joy had been banished because he could no longer pray to God and that very day the burden had grown too heavy to bear.

In the kindest tones, Paula told him he should have come to the Inn and reported everything immediately and that he was right now in tell-

ing her so frankly about it; he would never re-
gret it. Then she added he could promise Jörgli
ten francs as soon as the cross was again in her
possession.

"Ten francs!" repeated Moni, full of astonishment, for he remembered that Jörgli had wished
to sell it for only four. Rising, Moni said he
would go to Küblis that very day, and if he se-
cured the cross he would bring it up to the Inn
early the next morning. Now he ran off, able once
again to leap and run, for his heart was light,
the heavy load no longer weighing him down.
Once home, he tarried only long enough to stall
his brown goat and tell his grandmother he had
another errand to do; then he started full run
for Küblis. He found Jörgli at home and
poured out the story of what he had done. At
first Jörgli was greatly enraged but when he reflected that all was known and further conceal-
ment impossible, he brought out the cross and
asked, "Will she give me anything for it?"

"Yes, and now you can see for yourself, Jörgli, that by honest means you would have received ten francs at once, and in your lying way, only four."

Jörgli was astonished and regretted that he

had not gone straight to the Inn after he had picked up the cross in front of the door, for he had been much troubled by his conscience, and that would have been different the other way. But it was too late now. He passed over the cross to Moni, who hastened home with it as it was already well into the night.

CHAPTER V

MONI SINGS AGAIN

PAULA had left instructions that she should be awakened early in the morning, for she wished to be dressed and out when the goat boy came by the Inn, for she planned to deal directly with him. In the evening she had had a long interview with the innkeeper and came out of his room looking as if she must have arranged something very satisfactorily with him.

When the goat boy arrived with his flock in the morning, Paula already stood in front of the

Inn and called out to him: "Moni, can't you sing
even now?"

He shook his head. "No, I can't! I still cannot help thinking of Mäggerli and wondering
how much longer the little kid will be able to go
along with me. I can sing no more so long as I
live. Here is the cross!" Therewith he passed
over to Paula a little package, for his grandmother had wrapped the precious cross carefully
in three or four pieces of paper.

Paula pulled the cross from its wrappings and looked at it closely. It was really her own beautiful cross, set with the sparkling stones, entirely undamaged. "So, Moni," she said, "you have given me a great pleasure, for without you I certainly would never have seen my cross again. Now I will give you some pleasure. Go fetch Mäggerli out of the stall there. She belongs to you now!"

Moni stared at the young woman in astonishment, unable to understand her words. At last he stuttered, "But how—how can Mäggerli be mine?"

"How?" returned Paula, laughing. "Listen! Last evening I bought Mäggerli from the landlord and this morning I make you a present of the kid. Now can you sing again?"

"Oh! Oh! Oh!" exclaimed Moni, and ran like mad to the shed, drew out the little kid and took it up in his arms. Then running back, he stretched out his hand to Paula and exclaimed over and over again, "Thank you a thousand,

thousand times! God reward you! If only I could do you a favor!"

"Well then, let us see how a song sounds again!" suggested Paula.

On the instant Moni burst into singing and went on his way up the mountain with the goats, his jubilation ringing far down the valley, so that there was not a soul at the Inn who did not hear the happy sound, and many turned on their pillows and said: "The goat boy has fine weather once more!"

Everybody rejoiced that he sang again, for they had grown accustomed to his happy morning alarm, some rising at the sound of it and others turning to slumber again.

As Moni reached the first summit he saw Paula still standing in front of the Inn. He stepped near the edge and sang down to her as loudly as ever he could:

> "The flowers all come in the springtime,
>   The violet, rose and bluebell,
> And the sky is so bright and blue then
>   My gladness I scarcely can tell."

The whole day long Moni shouted for very joy. The goats were infected by his happiness and hopped and skipped around as though there were a great fête going on up there. And the sun shone so brightly and the herbage was so fresh after the long rain, and the little red and yellow flowers bloomed in such profusion it seemed to Moni that never before had the mountains, the valley, and all the world looked so beautiful. He would not allow his little kid out of his sight one moment the entire day. He plucked the finest herbs for it and fed it, saying over and over again:

"Mäggerli, good little Mäggerli, now you do not have to die! You are mine and you'll come up here with me to graze just as long as we live."

That evening as Moni came down, his resounding songs and yodels could be heard for miles around and after leading Blackie to her shed at the Inn, he took the little kid on his arm, for it was going home with him. Mäggerli made no ado about leaving her old home, but cuddled up close to the goat boy as if she knew protection lay there, for Moni had for a long time treated her more tenderly than her own mother.

Moni's grandmother did not know what to make of it when she heard Moni's song, and was still more puzzled when she saw him with Mäggerli on his shoulder. Although he shouted to her from the distance, "Mäggerli belongs to me now, Grandmother, she belongs to me!" it did not make the matter clear to her. First Moni ran to the stall and there near Brownie he made a fine soft bed of fresh straw, for he did not wish the little goat to be afraid in the new home. Tenderly he put the kid down and said, "There,

Mäggerli, now sleep soundly in your new home. Every day I'll make you a fresh little bed!"

At last Moni went to the wondering grandmother and as they sat at their evening meal he related the whole story to her from the very beginning, telling her of the three troubled days and the present happy outcome.

The grandmother listened silently and attentively and when he had concluded, she said earnestly, "Moni, as long as you live you must remember what has just happened to you. While you were making so much trouble for yourself by doing wrong in order that you might help the little creature, the good Lord would have come to Mäggerli's aid long before and He had found a way to make you happy as soon as you had done what was right. Had you confided in Him at the very first, all would have gone well. Now that the good Lord has helped you beyond what you have deserved, you must never forget it so long as you live."

"No, certainly I will never forget it!" declared Moni with passionate assurance. "I will always think: 'I must always do what is right before the good Lord; He will take care of the rest!'"

Before Moni could lay himself down to sleep

that night, he had to take another look in at the shed to assure himself that the little kid was really there and belonged to him.

As Paula promised, Jörgli received the ten francs; but he was not to escape so easily. When he came again to the Inn, he was taken before the landlord, who held the boy by the collar, gave him a good shaking and said in a threat: "Jörgli, Jörgli! never try again to bring my Inn into disgrace. If such a thing happens a second time, you will get out of my house in a way that will not please you. See, over there hangs a nice supple willow switch for just such cases. Now out with you, and remember!"

There was another consequence to Jörgli besides this. Whenever anything was lost at the Inn, all the servants cried out immediately, "Jörgli of Küblis has it!" And when next he came to the hotel they would all crowd around him and demand: "Give it up, Jörgli! Hand it over!" And if he assured them he had nothing and knew nothing about the lost article, they

would insist: "We know you! You can't fool us!"

In this way Jörgli had to defend himself against continual attacks and scarce had a peaceful moment, for when he saw anyone coming towards him he immediately feared he was coming to ask, "Have you found this, or that?" Jörgli never felt comfortable and many times said to himself, "Oh, that I had given up that cross on the spot! For the rest of my life I will never again keep anything that does not belong to me."

On the other hand, Moni never stopped singing and yodeling the whole summer long, for in all the wide world there was no one happier than this lad up on the mountains with his goats. Often as he stretched himself out on the Pulpit Rock in his contentment and gazed down into the sunlit valley below he recalled the time when he sat under the Rain Rock bereft of all joy. And always he said in his heart: "I know now how to act so that will never come about again.

I will not do anything that will prevent me looking happily up into the sky, because that will be
right before the good Lord."

If, however, Moni was lost in meditation too

long, some one or other of the goats would come
near, gaze at him in surprise and seek to bleat
him back into companionship. Often he did not
hear them for a long time, but when his own
Mäggerli needed him and called for him, then
he heard immediately and leaped off to meet her,
for his faithful little goat was and remained
Moni's dearest possession.